Billy Brown Bear and Friends

Short Stories, Fuzzy Animals, and Life Lessons

Norma MacDonald

Billy Brown Bear and Friends
Short Stories, Fuzzy Animals, and Life Lessons
Copyright ✻ 2016 Norma MacDonald

Published by: Find Your Way Publishing, Inc.
PO BOX 667
Norway, ME 04268 U.S.A.

www.findyourwaypublishing.com

ISBN-13: 978-0-9849322-5-2
ISBN-10: 0-9849322-5-9

First Edition

Library of Congress Control Number: 2016935754
Printed in the United States of America.

Dedication

This book is dedicated to all of the people trying to make the world a better place. You are making a positive difference!

"Everything we do, even the slightest thing we do, can have a ripple effect and repercussions that emanate. If you throw a pebble into the water on one side of the ocean, it can create a tidal wave on the other side."

~ **Victor Webster**

Table of Contents

About This Book

Welcome to our Karma for Kids Book Series. We are very grateful that you picked up this book. We believe together we can make a positive difference, one child at a time. We strive to instill important life lessons in the lives of young children. We are firm believers in Karma and think that if this simple Law of the Universe is taught to children at a young age, their lives will have the potential to be absolutely amazing.

We once knew a dog named Karma. She was a beautiful, yellow Labrador retriever. It wasn't until after she passed, at 11 years old (God bless her loyal soul.), that we realized just how fitting her name really was.

Karma is indeed a retriever.

Whatever we threw out, Karma was always happy to bring it back to us. It didn't matter what it was, she always brought it back. If we threw out garbage, she'd bring it back without question. If we threw out the most beautiful dog toy, she'd bring it back. It's the same in life. Whatever you send out, is what you will get back. Guaranteed. Every time. Our Karma for Kids Book Series hopes to instill this easy-to-understand Law of the Universe into the lives of children at a young age. The Universe wants to happily bring you all that your heart desires, and it will, effortlessly. But first you've got to throw out what you want it to bring back to you so that it can! Have fun with this and watch the magic happen. God bless!

Find all of Norma MacDonald's Karma for Kids Books at Amazon.com.

For more of our Karma for Kids books please visit us at:

www.karmaforkidsbooks.wordpress.com

Other books that we recommend to help children learn important life lessons:

Guaranteed Success for Kindergarten; 50 Easy Things You Can Do Today! By Marrae Kimball

Guaranteed Success for Grade School; 50 Easy Things You Can Do Today! By Marrae Kimball

The Secret Combination to Middle School: Real Advice from Real Kids, Ideas for Success, and Much More! By Marrae Kimball

Thank you!

Billy Brown Bear and Friends

Short Stories, Fuzzy Animals, and Life Lessons

Norma MacDonald

Chapter One

The Golden Rule

Billy Brown Bear was a bully. He was the biggest animal in the whole class and he picked on all the smaller animals. When Penny Puppy brought her tennis ball collection for show and tell, Billy Brown Bear threw them all over the fence. When Carl Crow taught the class how to build bird nests, Billy Brown Bear crushed them all with his big bear paws.

No other animals in the class liked Billy Brown Bear because he was so mean. The teacher, Mr. Lion, never yelled at Billy because he never saw him bully the other animals. Billy Brown Bear was sneaky. He only did mean things when Mr. Lion was not looking.

"Mr. Lion! Mr. Lion!" the class would call out, "Billy Brown Bear is at it again!"

But by the time Mr. Lion turned around, Billy Brown Bear was always sitting at his desk quietly.

One day, during lunch, Penny Puppy and Carl Crow were trading their snacks. Penny was giving Carl her milk bone because Carl had never tried one. Billy Brown Bear thought the milk bone looked delicious and decided that he wanted to try it first. He stomped his way over to the lunch table and snatched the milk bone right out of Penny's paws!

"Billy, give that bone back!" cawed Carl.

"No. I want this bone." Billy growled.

"That is not very nice Billy Brown Bear! You are a bully!" Penny barked.

Billy shoved the milk bone into his mouth and chewed it up. "That was delicious!"

Carl Crow and Penny Puppy frowned. "How would it make you feel if we did mean things to you, Billy?"

Billy Brown Bear let out a big belly laugh. He said, "You would never do mean things to me. I am much bigger than you. I could squash you under my paws just like I squashed Carl's crow nests!"

Carl and Penny decided to come up with a plan. If Billy wasn't going to stop bullying them, then they would give him a taste of his own medicine.

The next day, while Billy went to the bathroom down the hall, Carl pecked all of his pencils so that Billy couldn't use them, and Penny ate his homework. Mr. Lion wasn't even looking because he was eating an apple and reading the newspaper.

When Billy Brown Bear came back from the bathroom and noticed that his things were ruined he got so angry. He let out a big growl and the entire class gasped and stared at him.

"Billy please quiet down," Mr. Lion said from behind his newspaper.

But Billy was so angry that he started bullying the whole class. He unraveled Kyle Kitten's ball of yarn and threw it into the trash can. He ate up all of Mary Mouse's cheese. And then he turned to Penny and Carl. He started to stomp right toward them just as Mr. Lion finally looked up from his newspaper.

"Billy Brown Bear!" he shouted. "What do you think you are doing to my class?"

"Penny ate my homework and Carl pecked away at my pencils!" He held up a paw full of pencils.

Mr. Lion sighed and asked for Penny Puppy and Carl Crow to come up to the front of the class and apologize to Billy Brown Bear.

"I don't want to tell Billy I'm sorry because he made me lose my entire tennis ball collection!" cried Penny.

"I don't want to tell Billy I'm sorry because he stole the milk bone I was going to eat at lunch!" cried Carl.

"Well," said Mr. Lion, "that does not mean you should do mean things back to Billy, does it?"

"We just wanted him to know what it felt like to be bullied since he bullies all of us!"

Mr. Lion nodded along. "Billy," he said, "is it true that you bully my class?"

Billy Brown Bear couldn't even look at his teacher, he was so ashamed. "Yes, but—"

"How did it feel to be bullied?" Mr. Lion asked before he could give an excuse.

Billy Brown Bear was still looking down. "Bad."

"Class, do you know what the Golden Rule is?" Mr. Lion asked. The whole class shook their heads. "The Golden Rules states that you should treat others the way you want to be treated. That means if you want others to be nice to you, you should be nice to them. But that does not mean it is okay to be mean to someone just because they were mean to you. It's never okay to be mean. It doesn't feel nice to have someone be mean to you, does it?"

The class shook their heads.

"So Billy Brown Bear, can you say sorry for bullying the class and promise that it will not happen anymore?"

Billy Brown Bear, now knowing how it felt, said he was sorry. And he meant it.

"And Penny Puppy and Carl Crow, can you say you're sorry to Billy Brown Bear for bullying him back?"

Penny Puppy and Carl Crow said they were sorry.

"Now class, what is the Golden Rule?"

The class spoke all together, "It means you should treat other people the way you want to be treated."

Norma MacDonald

Chapter Two

The Leash of Lying

Penny Puppy had the same leash for her entire life. It was pink with purple polka dots. She thought it was pretty, but it was getting old and dirty. The bright pink didn't pop as much as it used to because of too many days at the dog park. Penny Puppy wanted a new leash very badly.

At the dog park, Penny noticed that a lot of the other puppies got new leashes for their birthday. She saw green leashes and blue leashes with glitter and stripes and other cool designs. It made her feel embarrassed that her pink and purple leash was so old!

Penny Puppy really wanted a new leash, but she didn't know how to ask for one. What if it hurt her parent's feelings that she no longer liked the leash they picked out for her? Penny decided it was best to just find a leash she liked and take it, no one would have to know.

While she was walking to school one day, she saw a beautiful blue leash with beads on it, and the best part was it was brand new! Penny knew she had to have that leash. It was sitting on a bench all alone, but there were two dogs over by the tree, it probably belonged to one of them. Penny decided that those dogs wouldn't miss their leash and when no one was looking, she took it and ran off to school.

At school, she had trouble paying attention to everything Mr. Lion was teaching. She kept thinking about her new leash. She was worried that someone saw her take it, and that she would get into trouble. Even at recess when her best friend Carl Crow wanted to play tag, she just couldn't have fun.

"What's wrong Penny?" asked Carl.

Penny put her tail between her legs and said, "Nothing, I just have a tummy ache." She didn't want to tell Carl about stealing the leash because she didn't want anyone to overhear. Penny was so scared that she would get caught.

At home that night she could barely eat her supper. Even though she was having her favorite chicken stew, her stomach was tied up in knots because of stealing the leash.

"What's wrong Penny?" asked her mom. She rubbed Penny's belly because that always helped Penny relax.

Penny didn't know what to tell her mom about what she had done that day, so she stayed silent and went to sleep in her big fluffy puppy bed. As Penny dozed off to sleep she began to dream.

She was in a big green grassy field with a bunch of other dogs. They were all comparing leashes and Penny was sporting her new stolen leash. All the dogs in the park admired it and gave her millions of compliments.

"What a beautiful leash!"

"Where can I get a leash like that?"

"How long have you had the beautiful leash?"

Penny didn't know how to answer any of their questions. She started feeling sick. Before she could say anything to the other dogs about her leash she heard vicious barking in the distance. The barks started to get louder and closer. On the horizon, she saw two big German shepherds with police hats running toward her. While all the other dogs in Penny's dream stared at the police dogs, she began to run as fast as she could away from them.

The police dogs were very fast, they continued to get closer and closer to Penny no matter how fast she ran. She ducked under benches, jumped over bushes, and tried to lose them by turning down an alley, but the police dogs were smarter than her, and one of them went around to the other end of the alley. She was stuck.

"What are you running for Penny Puppy?" One of the big police dogs asked.

"Is there something you are hiding?" Asked the second police dog.

Penny started to whimper.

Then she woke up. Her legs were tired and she was panting, she must have been running in her sleep! Her mom came into the room to check on her. She was crying so hard from the bad dream that she couldn't even speak, but she pointed to the corner of the room where she had buried the stolen leash under her toys.

Penny Puppy's mom went to the pile of toys and dug around until she found the beautiful blue leash with beads. She picked it up and inspected it, trying to remember where it came from. She concluded that the leash was new, but it was not one that she had bought for Penny.

"Where did you get this new leash?"

Poor Penny Puppy just could not keep lying. She confessed to her mother. "I took it from a park

17

bench while two dogs were off near the trees. It was pretty and new and I liked it, so I took it. I'm sorry!"

Penny Puppy whimpered and put her tail between her legs. She was so afraid that she was about to get yelled at because she knew she did something only bad dogs do. She didn't want to spend the rest of the night in the dog house, she preferred her comfortable bed inside. Penny Puppy just cried and cried, she felt so guilty!

"You know that is stealing? And stealing is wrong. If you see something you like, just ask. We can always figure out a way to work toward things that you want." said her mom.

Penny nodded and said, "I didn't want to hurt your feelings and make you think I didn't like the leash you bought for me."

"Penny, it is okay to have opinions about things, just be honest."

"I'm sorry! I won't steal anymore. I learned my lesson." Penny knew that it was better to be honest and not steal because it meant she wouldn't have nightmares about the police and it meant she wouldn't have to lie to her friends.

The next day, Penny Puppy brought the beautiful blue leash with beads back to the bench. The two dogs were sitting there waiting for the bus.

"I think this leash belongs to one of you. I took it the other day, I'm sorry." Penny handed the leash over. She had her tail between her legs again, getting ready for the dogs to be angry with her.

Instead of yelling, the two dogs thanked her so much for returning it. "This leash was a present when I graduated from school, I'm so happy you brought it back!"

Penny Puppy realized that just because something looked cool to her, that didn't mean she should take it. That leash was important to someone else. She didn't just take the leash, but she also took the wonderful memories the leash carried with it. Penny Puppy felt happy and free to no longer be distracted about the stolen leash and she was able to have a normal fun day at school!

Chapter Three

Mr. Lion was the coach of the school's soccer team. They practiced every Monday and Wednesday after school and played games on Friday. Everyone in the class was on the team. Carl Crow was on offense because he was so fast. Penny Puppy played defense because she was really good at getting the ball back up the field. Billy Brown Bear was the goalie because he nearly took up the whole net! Nothing could get past Billy Brown Bear!

The class really loved practicing, it was so much fun. Mr. Lion would take the soccer ball and run around the field while the whole team chased him trying to get. They would take turns seeing who could kick the ball the farthest.

Billy Brown Bear liked it best when everyone tried to score goals on him because no one ever could. He stopped every ball that was kicked his way. "I'm the best player on the entire team!" Billy Brown Bear boasted.

Carl Crow liked it best when the team did warm-up laps. They would run around the field, but no one was as fast as him. He always finished way ahead of everyone else. "I'm the best player on the entire team!" Carl Crow claimed.

Penny Puppy liked it best when players tried to get around her. She always got in their way and made it hard for them to shoot the ball at the goal. It was as if she was a brick wall! "I'm the best player on the entire team!" Penny Puppy protested.

Mr. Lion always told his players they were the best whenever he talked to them. He wanted to make sure everyone felt important and valued. But Mr. Lion didn't realize that everyone really thought they were the best. And better than everyone else.

During recess, Billy, Carl, and Penny took a soccer ball outside with them and kicked it around between them. Mr. Lion loved seeing his players outside practicing. It made him proud that they took the sport seriously and gave it their all. What Mr. Lion didn't know was that outside, while his players were practicing, they were also arguing!

"I'm going to score so many goals on Friday and that is the reason we will win. The team would be so bad if I wasn't on it," said Carl.

"That's not true; we will win because I will get in the way of the other team and steal the ball to pass to you. You wouldn't be able to score any goals if I wasn't on the team," said Penny.

"You're both wrong. We will win because I will stop the other team from scoring every time they try. They won't score any goals, so you won't have to worry about falling behind. If I wasn't on the team, you would have to score way more goals than you usually do," said Billy.

"Then I dare you to let the other team score, just so you can see how good I am!" shouted Carl.

"Well then I won't pass the ball to you if you think you can just score all the goals without my help!" shouted Penny.

"Yeah! Let's see how good you really are, Carl!" shouted Billy.

Just then the bell rang, signaling that recess was over. The three teammates went back inside their classroom. Mr. Lion continued his lesson about dinosaurs, but most of the class wasn't listening. Everyone was thinking about what would happen at the game on Friday if Billy Brown Bear didn't block any balls and if Penny Puppy stopped passing to Carl. Would the team still win?

When game time came on Friday everyone in the stands heard the rumors that the players might not try their hardest because of an argument over who was the best. The crowd was nervous, they wanted to see the team win.

Mr. Lion told the team to go out and play their best and everyone ran onto the field and took their positions. Billy Brown Bear in the goal, Penny Puppy on defense, and Carl Crow on offense. The whistle blew and everyone started scrambling for the ball.

Carl Crow got to it first and he ran straight up the middle of the field so quickly that the other team didn't stand a chance of catching him. He spun around the defenders and kicked the ball as hard as he could and it sailed right over the goalies head and into the net. The whole crowd cheered and Mr. Lion roared along with them. Penny Puppy turned around and looked at Billy Brown Bear, they nodded, the plan was on.

Next time, Carl Crow was not the first to the ball and the other team started dribbling toward Penny. She stopped them and passed the ball to Kyle Kitten instead of Carl Crow. Kyle wasn't as fast as Carl, so the other team got the ball before he could.

They kicked it way over Penny's head right toward the goal. Billy Brown Bear reached up to it, but didn't try his best, and the ball went into the goal. Everyone was shocked. That was the first time anyone had ever scored on Billy Brown Bear!

Carl Crow was very angry that his teammates were playing badly on purpose. He took his anger out on the ball, trying to get it into the goal as fast as possible. He pushed the other players out of his way and the referee blew the whistle. "Foul!"

The other team got a free kick and it sailed into the goal again!

Everyone watching the game started booing Billy Brown Bear. He didn't care though, he knew that he wasn't trying his best and if he was, neither of those goals would have gotten by him. Carl

Crow needed to know that he wasn't the only player on the team, though!

When halftime came they were losing 5 to 1, it was the worst game the team ever played. Mr. Lion gathered all the players up and gave them a pep talk. "It's okay team, we still have a chance to come back and win this game! Just work together!"

Carl Crow interrupted his coach and shouted at the team, "Just pass me the ball and I will score!"

"Now now, Carl, that isn't how a team plays! You need to have confidence in everyone around you," Mr. Lion said. The rest of the team nodded.

"But Billy Brown Bear can't block any of the balls booted his way! And Penny Puppy pretends that she can't pass to me!" Carl Crow was getting more and more mad every minute. He continued to shout, "I'm the best player on this whole team. If I wasn't playing, we wouldn't even have scored one goal!"

"Then don't play and find out," Mary Mouse squeaked.

"Fine!" Carl Crow sat down on the bench. All his feathers were ruffled and he crossed his wings.

When it was time for the second half, the team took to the field, except for Carl Crow. He stayed put on the bench. The crowd gasped when they saw this happen, Carl never sat on the bench!

When the whistle blew, just as expected, the other team got the ball and dribbled up the field. Penny Puppy stopped them and kicked it as far as she could up the field. Mary Mouse was there and without even realizing it, the ball bounced right off her nose and into the goal for the team's second point. The crowd cheered, but Carl Crow crossed his wings even tighter. He felt frustrated because the team was playing better without him.

The next kickoff, the other team kicked it hard right at the goal. They didn't want to take the chance of Penny stopping them again. This time, Billy Brown Bear caught it between his two big paws.

There was one minute left in the game and they were only losing by one point. The other team didn't score one goal in the entire second half.

"Mr. Lion, can I go back in now?" Carl Crow decided he would rather be playing with the team than pouting on the bench. Mr. Lion sent him back onto the field and everyone cheered.

As Carl ran onto the field he looked back at Penny and Billy and apologized for saying he was better than them. He realized that the only reason he could play as good as he did was because he had a team that was just as good.

During the last minute of the game, Penny stole the ball from the other team and passed it to Carl who was waiting by the sideline. He zig-zagged through players all the way up the field. The crowd started counting down, "5 - 4 - 3 - 2..."

Right as the last second came, Carl Crow kicked the ball and it flew like a dart right into the corner of the goal. He scored!

The team ran up to him and gave him a pat on the back. "Good job, Carl!" Carl smiled, but he knew he couldn't have scored that goal if it wasn't for the others. Everyone ran off the field to where Mr. Lion was standing on the sidelines. He was clapping and congratulating the team on coming back from a big point difference. Even though they didn't win, he was proud that they worked their hardest no matter what.

"Good job team!" said Mr. Lion. "I know the first half wasn't the best, but I am glad that you were all able to work together during the second half to tie up the game! How exciting was that?!"

Carl Crow stepped up and asked Mr. Lion if he could say something to everyone.

"I just want to say that I'm sorry," Carl began, "I shouldn't have said that I was the only player on the team who was valuable. I know goals are what give us points, but no one can score goals without a great team behind them. Billy Brown Bear is a great goalkeeper, without him playing his best, the other teams would score so many points. And Penny Puppy is a great defender, she makes sure the other team doesn't even get a chance to try to score. Everyone else is great too. I realize now that our team wouldn't be good if it wasn't for how well we all play together."

Mr. Lion applauded his speech. "Thank you, Carl! That is right! Teamwork is what makes us win games. Together, you are all the best player!"

Everyone cheered and jumped on top of Carl Crow to celebrate. At the bottom of the pile, he just laughed and laughed.

Norma MacDonald

Chapter Four

Rabbit Food

During lunch break, everyone liked to show off what snacks they brought from home. There were cookies and brownies and chips that everyone liked to brag about. Everyone loved the cookies and the brownies were just as good. They were sweet and gooey and filled with lots and lots of sugar. The chips were salty and crunchy and every time you ate one, you would want even more of them.

Mary Mouse was never included in the exchanging of snacks because no one wanted her carrots or red peppers or celery. She felt embarrassed that she was the only one eating vegetables for a snack. Everyone loved junk food and it was like a contest to see who had the tastiest snack. Mary Mouse never won that contest.

Billy Brown Bear always had brownies.

Carl Crow always had crackers.

Kyle Kitten always had cookies.

Penny Puppy always had Pop-tarts.

One day Mary Mouse decided that she wanted to be one of the classmates who had yummy snacks. The others always told her she was just eating rabbit food. But even Riley Rabbit had more delicious treats!

She went home and told her parents about all the snacks she could be having instead of all the fruits and vegetables they were packing up into her lunch box.

"Mom. Dad. Tomorrow, with my lunch, well… well, I was thinking that maybe instead of my usual snack, I could have a cup of chocolate pudding!" she suggested.

Her parents stared at her with wide eyes and open mouths. They were shocked that their little girl, who was always eating carrots, would want something different.

"Mary Mouse, what makes you want something different than what we usually give you?" asked her dad.

"And why something so unhealthy?" asked her mom.

"Because," said Mary Mouse, "because that's what all of my friends are eating! I am the only one who eats vegetables for snack and no one ever tells me how good it looks or how much they want some. Everyone thinks my snacks are disgusting!"

"Do you think your snacks are disgusting?" asked her parents.

"Well, I like carrots, but I also like chocolate pudding."

"Fine, tomorrow you can have pudding, but then it is back to the food groups that are nutritious and good for you. We don't want our little girl to get sick!"

Mary Mouse was so excited that she would be part of the snack comparison conversation tomorrow. She gave her mom and her dad both big hugs and kisses before going to sleep for the night.

When the morning came Mary Mouse jumped out of bed and scurried downstairs to the kitchen where her mom always packed up her lunches. There, on the counter, was her little lunch box. She peeked inside and saw one juice box, one sandwich, and under that was where her snack always lived. She pushed the sandwich aside, and there at the bottom of her lunch box was a container filled with chocolate pudding!

She jumped and clapped her little hands together. "Thank you, thank you, thank you, Mama Mouse!" She grabbed the lunch box and hurried out the door to catch her bus. The whole bus ride to school Mary Mouse could not stop smiling. Lunch time was going to be so great now that she could talk to her other classmates about what they were snacking on that day. For once she wouldn't be the one eating "rabbit food" and being made fun of.

When the bell rang, to signal that it was time for lunch, Mary Mouse sprang out of her seat and sprinted to the cafeteria. She was the first one to the table. Before pulling out her cup of chocolate pudding, she wanted to make sure everyone was there, but Kyle Kitten never showed up.

Everyone started pulling out their snacks. Again, Penny had Pop-tarts, Billy had brownies, and Carl had crackers. They started to barter with each other.

"I'll give you a cracker if you give me a bite of your brownie."

"How about two crackers for a bite of my brownie?"

"Done."

And then they would trade their snacks and indulge.

When everyone was deep into eating their sugary and salty snacks, Mary Mouse pulled out her cup of pudding without saying a word. All of a sudden everyone got quiet.

"What is that?!"

Mary looked up and saw that everyone was staring right at her and her pudding, just like she hoped would happen.

"Oh, this?" She pointed to her cup of pudding. "It's just a cup of delicious chocolate pudding that my mom packed in my lunch today."

"Wow!"

Mary didn't offer up any trades and she enjoyed the entire cup of pudding all by herself.

The next day, she begged her mom for one more day of pudding as a snack, and she agreed. At the lunch table, the same thing happened. But this time, Kyle Kitten AND Penny Puppy were absent.

"Where are Kyle and Penny?" asked Mary Mouse.

"They are both at home sick," said Billy Brown Bear.

"Yeah they both got the flu and have a fever," said Carl Crow.

Everyone continued to eat the snacks and lunches until it was time to go back to class.

The next day, Mary Mouse was back to eating carrots as her snack. She was sad that her time of fame had come and gone, but was happy that she, at least, got to feel what it was like to be popular at the lunch table.

But, much to her surprise, all of her friends at the lunch table were absent that day. Kyle Kitten wasn't there. Penny Puppy wasn't there. Carl Crow wasn't there. Billy Brown Bear wasn't even there! In fact, the only people in class were Mary Mouse and Riley Rabbit!

"Well," Mr. Lion said, "since most of the class is missing today, there is no use going on with the dinosaur lesson. You two can go have an extra hour of recess."

Mary Mouse was so excited to have more time to play outside and even more excited that none of her friends had to see her eating carrots again!

When she got home from school that night she told her parents everything. She told them that all of her friends were jealous of her pudding. She told them that everyone was sick. And best of all, she told them about the extra hour of recess!

"I wonder why all of your friends got sick," said her mom.

"You should ask them what their doctors told them," said her dad.

The next day Kyle and Penny were back, but Billy and Carl were still absent. When lunchtime came around, Mary planned to ask where they had been, but before she could even get the words out, she saw that Kyle had carrots as a snack!

"Kyle, are you eating carrots instead of cookies?!" she exclaimed.

Kyle pouted and said, "Yes. My doctor told me I got sick because I don't eat healthy food enough. My body hasn't been getting the nutrients that it needs. Now my mom insists that I eat vegetables as a snack."

"The same thing happened to me!" said Penny Puppy as she pulled an apple out of her lunchbox. "My doctor told me that I will feel have more energy, and fight off illnesses if I eat better foods."

Mary Mouse realized that her parents weren't trying to make her unpopular at the lunch table by making her eat healthy food, they were trying to take care of her! She felt so happy that her parents loved her so much that they still took care of her even when they weren't around. She didn't have to worry about getting sick and feeling bad because her parents were making sure she ate healthy foods.

Even if it meant having to eat vegetables.

Norma MacDonald

Chapter Five

You Can't Play With My Toys

Whenever it rained, recess would get canceled. It wasn't as fun to have inside play time instead of outside play time, but no one really complained. There were some pretty cool toys to play with inside the classroom. There were dollhouses, toy cars, and a huge bin of building blocks, just to name a few.

Kyle Kitten really loved the dollhouse with the most rooms. It was so tall that he had to stand on his hind legs to reach the top room. Whenever there was an indoor recess, Kyle was the first to that dollhouse. He also had a favorite doll to make live there.

No one else really bothered him about playing with the house, because they all had their favorite toys too.

One week it just would not stop raining. The class had to have indoor recess every single day. By Wednesday, all of the students were growing antsy. Everyone really missed being able to run around. During their playtime, Kyle was using the dollhouse, Billy and Carl were using the building blocks, Penny was playing with a racecar, and Mary was reading a book in the corner just like she always did.

When she came to the end of her book she decided she would join the others to play.

First she went over to Penny Puppy to join in on the racecar track being built.

"Hi Penny, can I help you build that racecar track?"

"I'm almost finished and I don't need help. This is only a one-person game."

Mary left Penny alone and went over to Billy and Carl who were building a giant pyramid of blocks.

"Hi, Billy Brown Bear. Hi, Carl Crow. Can I help build that pyramid?"

"No, you don't know what the plan is and we already worked so hard on it," said Billy.

"Yeah," said Carl, "it wouldn't be fair for you to join in now and act like you helped build the whole thing!"

Mary left them alone and went over to Kyle Kitten who was playing with his favorite dollhouse.

"Hi, Kyle. Do you mind if I join in on the dollhouse game?"

"No way! This is my favorite dollhouse, I play with it every day. Go play with a different one."

"But it wouldn't be as fun to play by myself and everyone else already said no."

"Too bad, this is my dollhouse and I said you can't play with it."

Mary wasn't one to argue so she left him alone and went back to her corner. She didn't have another book to read so she just sat and watched all of her friends playing without her.

The next day it was raining again and Mary Mouse was determined to play with her friends during indoor recess. When the bell rang she ran over to the racecars and started building a track.

"What are you doing?" asked Penny Puppy. "That's my toy."

"I just thought I could play with it today since you did yesterday," said Mary.

"Well I've been playing with it all week and you haven't so just go play with something else!"

Again, Mary didn't like to argue, so she scurried over to the blocks.

Billy Brown Bear had just dumped the pile of blocks out of their bin and onto the floor. Carl was sorting through them organizing them by color.

Mary Mouse joined in organizing the blocks.

"What are you doing?" Carl Crow asked confused.

"These blocks are our toys," said Billy Brown Bear.

"Well since you haven't started building yet, today, I thought I could join in and help out this time."

"We have been building stuff with the blocks every day this week and you haven't. You aren't part of the block building club," said Billy.

"Yeah," said Carl, "just go play with something else!"

Again, Mary left them alone and scurried over to the dollhouse.

Kyle just sat all the dolls down at the dinner table. Mary grabbed a doll he wasn't using from the toy chest and shoved the doll into one of the empty chairs.

"What are you doing?" asked Kyle Kitten.

"I wanted to play dolls with you today since I didn't get a chance to yesterday."

"I always play with this dollhouse, it practically belongs to me!"

"But it really belongs to all of us since it's in the classroom. I just think it would be nice if you let me play," Mary squeaked out.

"Well someone else can let you play, not me."

Mary again went back to her corner and watched as all of her friends played with the toys.

Mr. Lion noticed that Mary was sitting alone, with nothing to do, so he went over to check on her.

"What's wrong Mary Mouse?"

"No one will share the toys with me, so I'm just watching them instead."

Mr. Lion frowned. "Well that is not very nice, is it?"

Mary shrugged. "I don't mind." She didn't want anyone to get in trouble.

Mr. Lion decided to stop playtime early and call the class back to their seats. When everyone was back at their desks he began to talk about sharing.

"Sharing is very important. We have lots of really cool toys in this classroom, but if you don't let everyone get a turn to play, then they won't get to have fun! It's not very nice to keep something from one of your friends just because you want it all to yourself. Remember the Golden Rule? Well, that goes for sharing too."

Everyone realized that by not letting Mary Mouse join in on the fun, they were being mean.

"I'm sorry Mary, I know I would be sad if I didn't get to play with blocks," Billy Brown Bear said.

"Me too," said Carl Crow.

"And I could have used help on that race track, I'm sorry I didn't let you play with me," said Penny Puppy.

Kyle also apologized. "I know you all let me use the dollhouse, all the time because I like it so much, but that doesn't mean I should be the only one playing with it. I'm sorry Mary Mouse, I wasn't very nice to you."

Mary Mouse forgave everyone and they all went back to playtime together. They discovered that sharing can be a lot of fun too!

Norma MacDonald

Chapter Six

Ask For Help

Mr. Lion finally finished his lesson on the dinosaurs. Now it was time for the class to do their final projects on what they had learned. Each student had to make a poster of a different dinosaur and include facts about it.

Billy Brown Bear picked T-Rex because it was big like him.

Carl Crow picked Pterodactyl because they had wings.

Penny Puppy picked Triceratops because she thought their horns looked like dog bones.

Mary Mouse picked Stegosaurus because she thought the spikes were cool.

Kyle Kitten didn't know what to pick.

At lunch, everyone was talking about their projects and about the cool things they had learned so far.

"Did you know that girl T-Rexes were bigger than boys?!"

"That's not as cool as a giant flying dinosaur!"

"Well guess what? Triceratops only ate plants even though they had those giant horns!"

"Giant horns are nothing! Stegosaurus had tail spikes that could be three feet long!"

Kyle Kitten just ate his lunch silently and let the others debate about who had the coolest dinosaur. Back in class, they had research time. Everyone had books opened to read up on their dinosaurs. Some were even already putting facts onto a poster board. Kyle flipped through the books trying to decide what to pick. Finally, he settled onto Iguanodon because the picture looked sort of like Godzilla.

At home that night, he told his parents that he would be doing a project about the Iguanodon and that he would be in his room working on it. In his little room, he started to design what his poster would look like, but he couldn't decide how to include facts and a picture, and also make it pretty and colorful. He didn't want a boring poster, but he was not as creative as the others.

In school, the next day, everyone was talking about what their posters were going to look like. Penny Puppy put glitter on hers and Billy Brown Bear made a cardboard cutout of a T-Rex!

Kyle Kitten was very nervous about his project. He wanted to get a good grade but didn't think he would be able to do as well as his friends.

The night before the project was due, Kyle Kitten couldn't fall asleep. He stayed up in his room trying to think of ideas to make his poster better and he tried to think of more creative things to do to it. He grew more and more frustrated until finally he just started to cry.

The sound of him crying woke up his dad and he came in to check on Kyle.

"What's the matter, son?"

"I have this stupid project due tomorrow and I just can't do it!"

The poster board was on the ground with nothing on it. There was a box of crayons on his desk and a glue stick next to them. He printed out a picture of an Iguanodon and had an index card where he wrote down all of the facts:

1. The Iguanodon was discovered in the 19th century
2. They ate plants
3. They have thumb spikes—but no one knows why!

Kyle Kitten continued crying. His dad gave him a big hug and said, "You know, Kyle, you should have just asked for help."

"All of my friends were doing their projects alone. I didn't want to be a failure and have to have my dad help me. That's embarrassing!"

Kyle's dad rubbed his head, "Asking for help doesn't make you stupid, it makes you smart! Only the smartest people know when it's time to ask for help."

"Really?" Kyle asked.

"Really," said his dad.

"Dad...can you help me with my project?"

"Of course!"

Kyle Kitten and his dad stayed up the rest of the night gluing things onto the poster and making colorful borders with the crayons. It may not be glitter, or a cardboard cutout, but Kyle was very proud of his work.

When it was his turn to present, the next day in class, he stood in front of the class and said, "This is my poster with facts about the Iguanodon. There are a lot of cool things about this dinosaur, my favorite being its thumb spike. But what this project really taught me was that it's okay to ask for help. I learned all about this dinosaur after having a hard time picking one, and then I had a hard time making a cool poster. I didn't want my poster to be boring and not creative, but I didn't know what to do. That's when my dad came and told me that if you ask for help, it really means you're smart, not dumb. He said it takes a very smart person to know when to ask for help. I think that Iguanodons probably asked for a lot of help because they traveled in herds. And that is my presentation."

The whole class clapped and Mr. Lion gave him a pat on the back and said, "Well done. I couldn't have said it any better myself. Thanks for your help." Then he patted Kyle on the shoulder, in approval, before sending him back to his desk to listen to the next presentation.

Afterword

Thanks again for picking up this book! You are participating in making our world a better place.

For more of our Karma for Kids books please visit us at:

www.karmaforkidsbooks.wordpress.com

Find Norma MacDonald and her books online at Amazon.com.

Other books that we recommend to help children learn important life lessons:

Billy Brown Bear and Friends: Short Stories, Fuzzy Animals, and Life Lessons By Norma MacDonald

Guaranteed Success for Kindergarten; 50 Easy Things You Can Do Today! By Marrae Kimball

Guaranteed Success for Grade School; 50 Easy Things You Can Do Today! By Marrae Kimball

The Secret Combination to Middle School: Real Advice from Real Kids, Ideas for Success, and Much More! By Marrae Kimball

If you have ideas for stories, please feel free to send them to:

Melissa Eshleman

Find Your Way Publishing, Inc.

PO Box 667

Norway, ME 04268

Melissa@findyourwaypublishing.com

Thank you!

www.ingramcontent.com/pod-product-compliance
Lightning Source LLC
Chambersburg PA
CBHW071341130626
46556CB00004B/1978